KINGDOM
The Hidden Gemstone

Written by Michelle Mohrweis

Illustrated by Dante Gabriel Hookey

Collins

Chapter 1

It's cleaning day at the Feather Quill antique shop, which means I'm daydreaming about adventure. Maybe not the best idea while balancing on a ladder, but whatever.

"OK, next we need the books with orange spines," says my cousin, Samara. She waits below me, tapping a finger against her notebook. Samara keeps track of *everything* in her notebook.

I rise on my toes, reaching for a book on the highest shelf. The ladder wobbles, but I'm not afraid. I, Cleo MacGuffin, am an adventurer climbing a towering cliff towards the sky and …

The door bangs open.

I grab the shelf to steady myself as Mateo, prince of the Kingdom of Pages, runs inside.

"I need your help!" he cries, clutching a newspaper. "Mum wants me to go on a quest!"

GEMSTONE OF FIXING
HIDDEN IN
FORGOTTEN FOREST!

A quest? Excitement buzzes from my fingers to the tips of my toes.

"That's amazing!" I cry.

"No, no, no!" moans Mateo. He holds out the newspaper. "It's *not* amazing. I have to find this!"

Even from high up on the ladder, I can read the massive headline: *Gemstone of Fixing hidden in Forgotten Forest!*

"That sounds fun," says Samara.

Mateo throws the newspaper aside. "Neither of you get it. It's dangerous. I don't want to go! Besides, we keep getting complaints about rubbish in the forest. It's filthy there!"

Sometimes I forget Mateo doesn't like adventure the way Samara and I do. I don't really understand it, but he's my friend, and he's upset, which means I need to comfort him.

"I'm sorry," I say, scrambling to think of when I've felt similar. "I get it. My aunt always makes us clean the antique shop and I despise cleaning. It's frustrating! But I feel bad if I say no because she lets me stay here all summer."

Mateo scowls. "What's that have to do with my problem?"

My stomach drops. Did I … just make him *more* upset?

I rock on my feet, back and forth, heel to toe. I rock so hard that the ladder rocks with me.

Why did that make him angry?

When Samara and I get upset, we share stories to comfort each other, and it always makes us both feel better. But now Mateo is glaring at me and …

"Cleo, watch out!" yells Samara.

The ladder tips.

The ground races
towards me.

I fall with
a tremendous **CRASH**!

For a moment, I lay
stunned on the ground.
Am I OK?

"Ow," sniffles Samara.

I might be fine, but
Samara isn't. She's sitting
on the ground beside me,
holding her arm as she
blinks back tears.

"Are you OK?" Mateo
asks Samara.

She shakes her head.

Chapter 2

I need to say something, apologise, or check on her, but my words feel stuck. All I can manage is, "My aunt's next door. She can help."

Mateo helps Samara up, then frowns at the fallen ladder before leading her out of the door.

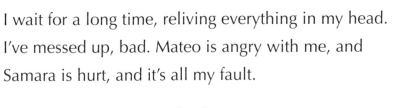

I wait for a long time, reliving everything in my head. I've messed up, bad. Mateo is angry with me, and Samara is hurt, and it's all my fault.

There must be a way to fix things.

That's when I notice Mateo's newspaper.

Oh! I have an idea.

I grab the newspaper, scanning the article.

GEMSTONE OF FIXING HIDDEN IN FORGOTTEN FOREST!

The Gemstone of Fixing has been spotted in the Forgotten Forest! This stone fixes any problem and heals any injury. Adventurers everywhere hope to find it.

That's it! I'll find the gemstone and give it to Mateo to help with his quest. And use it to fix Samara's arm too!

I tuck the newspaper under my arm and run out of the shop.

It's loud outside on the city streets, a wave of
noise ready to sweep me away. Carts rattle
along the cobblestones. People shout greetings.
Horses whinny.

This many noises are always hard to handle, but it
doesn't matter how much it hurts my head, not when
I'm on a mission.

I grit my teeth, cover my ears, and march onwards.

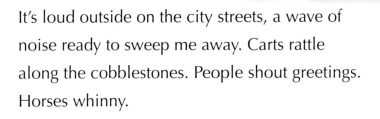

Chapter 3

Thankfully, it's quieter outside the city gates. I hurry as fast as I can, remembering the way Samara held her hurt arm.

But when the Forgotten Forest comes into view, I skid to a stop.

Wow!

The trees spread out like an ocean of green, stretching into the horizon. I climb down a hill and step into the forest, feeling like I've entered another world.

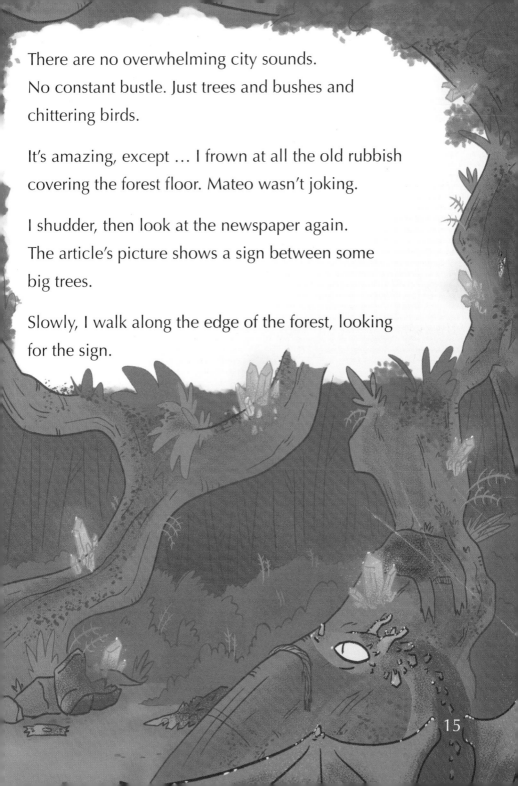

There are no overwhelming city sounds.
No constant bustle. Just trees and bushes and
chittering birds.

It's amazing, except … I frown at all the old rubbish
covering the forest floor. Mateo wasn't joking.

I shudder, then look at the newspaper again.
The article's picture shows a sign between some
big trees.

Slowly, I walk along the edge of the forest, looking
for the sign.

15

I spot it between two oak trees, with grass growing around its base and rubbish scattered around it.

And look! A riddle is written on the worn-out wood.

To find the stone
that shines so bright,
look to the ones
without much height.

I rock on my feet quickly, feeling both excited and a little guilty. I shouldn't be excited – I'm only here because I hurt my friends.

But I love riddles.

A riddle means the start of a quest, and a quest means adventure, and how can I not be excited about that?

Back and forth I rock.

Heel to toe.

Heel to toe.

As I rock, I notice that most of the trees tower over me, rising high into the air like giants grasping at the sky. But, nearby, sandwiched between a worn-out backpack and an empty can, I spot a small sapling.

I gasp, rocking harder. There's another sapling just a little further along!

The riddle must be talking about the saplings!

I follow them, heart racing. Once I find the gemstone and heal Samara, surely Mateo won't still be upset with me.

Though, I still don't really get why he was angry with me. Sometimes, the rules of what to do and say are so confusing, like there's a secret code everyone understands except me.

It's frustrating.

In that moment, I wonder if the Gemstone of Fixing can help me too.

I speed up, even more eager to find it.

The trees thin out as I go,
until I step around a huge
oak and find myself
beside a massive tower.
There's another sapling
right at the base of it, so
I reach for the door.

It creeeeeeeaks open.

22

I look cautiously inside. My eyes snap to the centre of the room, where a massive, shining diamond sits on a pedestal.

The Gemstone of Fixing!

I run over, barely daring to believe it, and reach out …

WHOOOSH!

A net sweeps me into the air! I struggle against
the criss-crossed rope, but it's no good. I'm trapped,
dangling a metre above the gemstone.

From the shadows nearby, somebody laughs.
"Another careless adventurer fell for my trap."

"Let me go!" I shout. I squirm against the net, trying to see who's there, but only manage to flip myself upside down.

"Oh no," says the figure, stepping forward. "I can't have you messing up the forest more." Lantern light illuminates an angry-looking girl.

"*Please* let me go!" I beg.

"No," she snaps. Then she reaches out and pulls a lever on the wall.

A trapdoor opens.

The net gives way and I fall … down, down, down into darkness.

Before I can shout, I hit the ground.

Oof!

Luckily, I land on a soft pile of dirt, sending up a cloud
of dust. I'm in a cold, dark room, with nothing but
a single torch on the wall and a small door beside it.

When I tug at the door, it doesn't budge.

It's locked.

Chapter 5

Even though I always claim I'm brave – that I'm Cleo MacGuffin, adventuring enthusiast! – right now I feel so small.

What kind of friend am I? I upset Mateo, hurt Samara, and didn't even get the gemstone. Today is the *worst*.

I sniffle, then start rocking on my feet.
Normally the back-and-forth motion calms me, but I'm too upset.

My head feels stuffy. My eyes hurt. Tears roll down my cheeks, and I hate that I'm crying but I can't stop. Not when my head is buzzing, and everything feels like too much.

I almost don't hear it when the door creaks open.

"Psssst … Cleo!"

"Mateo?" I whisper.

Sure enough, Mateo and Samara peek in through the newly unlocked door.

"Wh-what are you doing here?"

"We were worried! You went off by yourself, and the newspaper was gone, and you can't resist an adventure, so we knew you went looking for the gemstone!" says Samara, her words a whirlwind. "We came to find you."

"We followed your trail, and saw you get caught," adds Mateo.

"You came after me, even though it's dangerous?" I whisper.

"You're our friend," responds Mateo.

I turn to Samara. "Even though I hurt you?"

Samara holds out her bandaged arm, with a smile. "I'm OK, really! It only hurts a little."

I look back at Mateo. "But you were angry with me."

Mateo kicks at the dirt, looking away. "I'm sorry about that."

I hesitate, then add, "I'm sorry I upset you."

"It's OK," replies Mateo with a shrug. "I thought you were trying to one up me, like my brother does. But Samara explained that sharing stories is how you show you care. I just didn't understand."

Warmth floods my chest, pushing away my sadness.

Mateo may not be autistic like me, and he might not always understand how I do things, but he's willing to try. That means a lot.

Maybe I can do the same.

"Thanks," I say. "Later, can you tell me about things you do to show you care? I want to understand you too!"

Mateo nods.

"Great," laughs Samara. She claps her hands, then winces. "Ow! Anyway, shouldn't we go?"

I follow my friends out of the door and up the stairs beyond. We freeze at the top.

The girl stands between us and the door, facing away from us. She's talking to a potted fern. "Maybe if I prune your dead leaves, you'll get better," she coos at it.

Good, she's distracted.

We creep towards the door, nice and slow. We're almost there when …

Chapter 6

CREAAAAK! Samara steps on a loose floorboard.

"You!" the girl spins around. "How dare you try to escape!"

She lunges for the wall and yanks on a lever.
Heavy metal bars crash down in front of the door.

"Run!" I shout. We turn, bolting for the tower stairs, but the girl blocks our way.

"The lift!" suggests Samara. We dive into the lift and pull the lever. Up and up we go.

"Now what?" asks Mateo, as we emerge onto the rooftop.

I look around for anything we can use to escape. A rope? A ladder? There's nothing but a group of potted plants.

The girl emerges from the staircase, fists clenched.

"Stop!" I shout. "Or the tomatoes bite the dust!"
I hold a potted plant – a bush full of mini tomatoes –
over the edge of the tower.

"No!" gasps the girl. "Not Fred! He just
started fruiting."

"Then let us go," demands Samara.

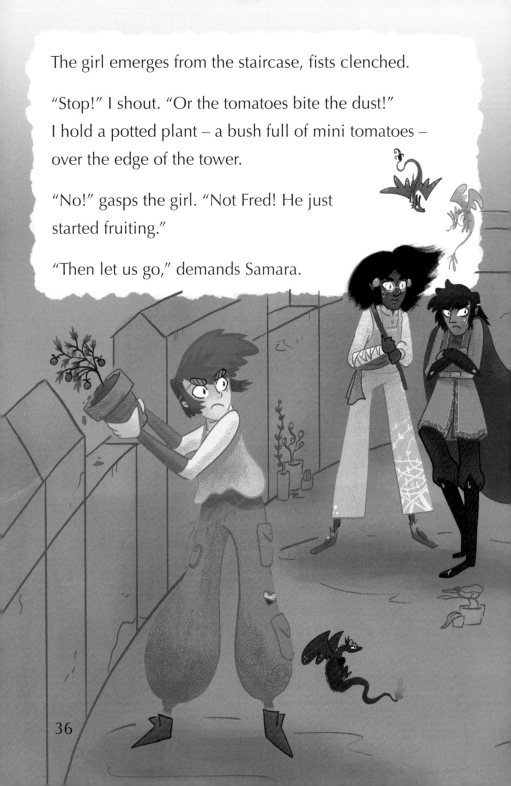

Mateo frowns. "Actually … tell us why you're capturing adventurers first."

The girl hesitates.

I tip the pot slightly, so a little dirt tumbles out.

"Fine!" cries the girl, taking a big step back.
"I'm Willow, and my mum is the forest ranger. Mum went to help my grandma while she's ill and I'm in charge until she's back. Only, adventurers keep leaving their rubbish everywhere. Mum's going to come back to a disaster!"

"So you decided to … capture them?"
asks Samara, pulling out her notebook from her bag.
She reaches for a quill pen, then winces and stops.

Willow blushes and stares at the ground.
"Most adventurers come searching for
the gemstone, so I made a fake one and
set up my trap. I don't plan to hurt anyone,
just scare them so they leave our forest alone."

I glance over the edge of the tower. Empty food packets,
crumpled maps and broken boots litter the forest floor.

A lump rises in my throat. Willow must be so frustrated trying to take care of the forest while others spoil it.

I hum and rock on my feet, trying to think.

Back and forth.

Heel to toe.

Heel to toe.

"There must be a better way to stop the rubbish," I declare.

Chapter 7

"You could ask for an audience with the prince," suggests Prince Mateo, with a grin. "I hear he's friendly. He can write a new law to protect the forest."

Samara giggles and elbows Mateo in the side. "Or you can organise a community clean-up day."

"Yeah!" I exclaim. I rock harder, thinking of more ideas. "What if you ask the newspaper to do a story about how the rubbish is harming the forest? Maybe people don't know."

RUBBISH PROBLEM!

"Those are great ideas," Willow says, blushing.

"If we help you, will you stop capturing adventurers?" asks Mateo.

Willow nods. "I shouldn't have started in the first place. I was just so upset."

"I get it. I'd be upset too," I agree, handing back the tomato plant. "Sorry they aren't respecting your forest."

"We'll change that," says Samara. She winces again as her arm bumps against her side.

Oh no … I never completed the quest. The Gemstone of Fixing is a fake, and I've no way to heal Samara.

"I wish the gemstone was real," I sigh, mournfully.

"About that – " Willow pulls out a small, seedlike stone and holds it up. "Mum found this in the forest. She says she uses it to fix things, but I've never been able to get it to work. Still, you can try it."

She hands it to me, and I hold it over Samara's arm.

I squeeze my eyes shut and focus. My fingers tingle. The gemstone warms in my grip. "Is it working?"

Samara shrugs. "I can't tell … but it's OK. I'll heal eventually."

"But you can't take notes!" I cry.

"True," Samara sighs. She glances at Willow and explains. "I'm ADHD, and writing everything down helps me remember things better."

An idea hits me then. Maybe the gemstone didn't help, but that doesn't mean *I* can't. "I'll take notes for you," I blurt out. "Just until your arm heals."

"Oh!" giggles Samara. "That'll be great."

I giggle too, relieved. As I squeeze my hand around the gemstone, I remember my thoughts from earlier.

Now I realise – I don't need the gemstone to help me either. There's nothing wrong with me.

Sometimes I'll have to make an effort to be a good friend, and sometimes my friends will have to make an effort to understand me, but that's OK. That's part of friendship.

I give the stone back to Willow.

"Come on," I say, rocking on my feet. "Let's think of more ideas while we start cleaning!"

"I'll get my mum," says Mateo thoughtfully. "I can show her all the rubbish people leave behind on their quest for the gemstone."

"Cleo, let's write down some ideas," proposes Samara, shoving her notebook at me. "Let's see … new laws … newspaper … community day – "

"Thank you!" cries Willow. "It's been so hard trying to take care of this place all alone."

"We're here to help now!" I say.

And so, as the sun sets on the Forgotten Forest, we get to work.

Guide to friendship

Be a good listener, and let your friends know how they can listen to you!

Help others the best ways *you* can.

Everyone messes up! It's how you handle it that matters.